Amelia Bedelia & FRIENDS

Mind Their Manners

Amelia Bedelia

& FRIENDS

Mind Their Manners

me

by **Herman Parish**

pictures by **Lynne Avril**

Greenwillow Books
An Imprint of HarperCollins Publishers

Library of Congress Control Number: 2020952190

ISBN 978-0-06-296190-7 (hardback)—ISBN 978-0-06-296189-1 (paperback)

21 22 23 24 25 PC/LSCH 10 9 8 7 6 5 4 3 2 1

First Edition

 Greenwillow Books

For my sisters, Mary and Fredda,
who owe their manners to Miss DeMint—H. P.

To Chloe and Jeff,
who have wonderful manners
(plus they learned Touch It Once,
and Do It Now!)—L. A.

Amelia Bedelia

Finally

Joy

Clay

Heather

Cliff

Wade

Dawn

Skip

Angel

Penny

Contents

Chapter 1: Smoke & Mirrors & Manners 1

Chapter 2: First Impressions Last 11

Chapter 3: Meet and Greet 21

Chapter 4: Candy Is Dandy? 28

Chapter 5: His Creases Have Creases 36

Chapter 6: From the Outside In 53

Chapter 7: Volcanoes Are a Blast! 63

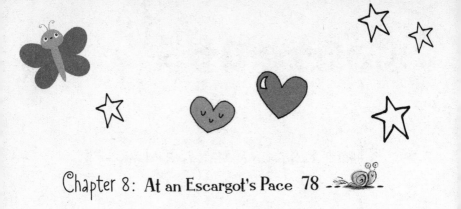

Chapter 8: At an Escargot's Pace 78

Chapter 9: Small Talk, Big Results 100

Chapter 10: Killed by Kindness 115

Chapter 11: Say You're Sorry 122

Chapter 12: I Scream, You Scream 131

Chapter 1

Smoke & Mirrors & Manners

UHH-*OHH!* UHH-*OHH!*

"Fire drill!" shouted Cliff. The fire alarm at Oak Hill Elementary sounded different from alarms at every other school. UHH-*OHH!* UHH-*OHH!*

It sounded like something very big had gone very wrong. It blared like one giant UHH-*OHH!* It was telling

UHH-OHH!!

UHH-OHH!!

everyone to get outside as quickly as possible. Amelia Bedelia and her friends knew exactly how to do that, since their school had fire drills often.

"Everyone lined up?" asked Cliff. His classroom job this month was Fire Marshall.

"Aye aye," said Clay, the current Assistant Fire Marshall. He handed Cliff the clipboard with the attendance list on it. That way Cliff could check off each student as they filed outside.

Mrs. Shauk, their teacher, was beaming. "Bravo," she said as her class calmly exited the building. "This drill is going like clockwork."

The only clockwork Amelia Bedelia had seen was inside her father's collection of antique pocket watches and timepieces up in their attic. She hoped this fire drill did not look anything like that complicated heap of gears and teeth and springs.

No matter what, she was going to remember this fire drill forever. For the very first time in her life, Amelia Bedelia had managed to be first in line. Quite an achievement, considering that her desk was in the back of the classroom, in the very last row. Luckily, she had overheard Mrs. Roman talking about a fire drill when she dropped off the morning attendance in the main office. So when she returned

to class, she'd stayed at the pencil sharpener in the front of the room, sharpening and re-sharpening her pencils until they were reduced to nubs.

As soon as the fire drill alarm went off, Amelia Bedelia had jumped, even though she'd been waiting for it. Covering her ears, she'd walked quickly to start forming a line.

Clay tried to get in front of Amelia Bedelia.

"Hey, I got here first," she said to him.

"I'm on important business," said Clay.

"Me too," said Amelia Bedelia. "It's important

4

to exit the school calmly and quickly, and I can lead everyone out." And she started to do just that, walking in the direction of the exit.

"There is no real fire," said Clay, once they were outside the school.

"Even more reason to let me be first," said Amelia Bedelia.

"No way," said Clay. "You're not the Assistant Fire Marshall. I am."

He stepped in front of Amelia Bedelia and shoved her behind him with his elbow.

"You can't push me," said Amelia Bedelia, glaring at him.

"I just did," said Clay, giving her another shove.

"Class!" said Mrs. Shauk. "Behave!"

"Hey, Clay, that's no way to treat a lady," said Angel.

"So what? Amelia Bedelia is no lady," said Clay.

"What did you say?" asked Mrs. Shauk.

What did you say?!?

The question had an immediate effect. Clay's eyes grew wide, but Mrs. Shauk's were even wider. Once again, Mrs. Shauk had lived up to her nickname: the Hawk. Their teacher spotted everything, missing no detail, even during a fire drill. Clay felt like a juicy rabbit looking up to see a hawk

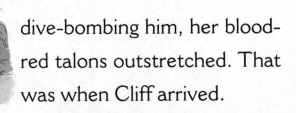

dive-bombing him, her blood-red talons outstretched. That was when Cliff arrived.

"Mrs. Shauk," interrupted Cliff, just in the nick of time. "You need to let this line move to our meeting spot!"

"Right you are, Cliff," said Mrs. Shauk as Amelia Bedelia continued to lead the class to their meeting place near the bus circle.

"Now," said Mrs. Shauk, "I believe we were just determining whether or not Amelia Bedelia is a lady."

"Of course she isn't," said Cliff. "She's just a girl."

Mrs. Shauk's eyes grew wider and wider. Amelia Bedelia was worried that

Mrs. Shauk's eyes were going to fall out of her head and roll down the school driveway. The very thought made her close her own eyes and rub them gently.

"Gentlemen," said Mrs. Shauk. "I think this calls for a discussion after school today."

"Weren't you happy with the drill?" asked Cliff.

"The fire drill went fine— not our best, just fine," said Mrs. Shauk. "But as they say, where there's fire, there is smoke."

"Don't you mean where there's smoke, there's fire?" asked Clay. "That's what my dad always says."

"Oh, there is no fire at Oak Tree Elementary," said Mrs. Shauk. "But there is a quite a bit of smoke to clear away, gentlemen. Quite a bit."

Amelia Bedelia stood between Cliff and Clay. She felt terrible. They were her friends. And now they were in trouble because of her. Amelia Bedelia looked at them. "I'm sorry you have to

be gentlemen and stay after school,"
she said. She shrugged. "But just so you
know, being a lady is no picnic either."

"Picnic," said Mrs. Shauk. "What a
delightful idea, Amelia Bedelia. But in
the meantime, Cliff and Clay, remember
to report to me after school today.
Now, everyone back inside—calmly and
quickly!"

Chapter 2

First Impressions Last

When Amelia Bedelia and her friends got to their classroom the next morning, they were surrounded by the evidence of Cliff and Clay's detention. Large whiteboards lined all four walls. At the very top of each board, the class recognized the distinctive handwriting of the Hawk. She had written:

I will be kind to others.

On each board, the same sentence was repeated over and over in two different styles of penmanship, Clay's block print and Cliff's sloppy scrawl.

I will be kind to others.
I will be kind to others.

In case there was any doubt, two boards were signed by Clay. The other two were signed by Cliff. Dawn, who loved math, blurted out, "Hey, Cliff and Clay each copied that sentence one hundred times!"

Amelia Bedelia thought about the courtroom and lawyer shows that her parents loved to watch. Was this what it meant when someone got sentenced?

Did the guilty person have to write the same sentence over and over for ten years? For twenty years? For the rest of their life?

"First, let me congratulate all of you on an exceptional fire drill yesterday, despite our challenges," said Mrs. Shauk as she erased the whiteboards. "Fortunately, you also brought something else to my attention." She finished with a flourish of her eraser and turned to face the class.

"Tell me the truth," said Mrs. Shauk. "How many of you think that being a lady or a gentleman, or acting with kindness and courtesy, is old-fashioned and only for grown-ups?"

Amelia Bedelia and her

friends looked at one another. This seemed like a trick question, and not one of them wanted to answer it.

"It appears that many of you think that being respectful depends on your age," continued the Hawk. "But just because you can drive a car and vote does not make you a lady or a gentleman. Acting like a lady or a gentleman is a skill that must be learned at all ages. It's only good manners."

"So we don't have to be real ladies or gentlemen as long as we act like them?" asked Penny.

"That doesn't make any sense," said Chip. "You are what you act like."

"Manners are so confusing," said Rose. "I never know if I'm doing the right thing or if people are laughing at me behind my back."

"It's bad manners to laugh behind someone's back," said Teddy.

"If others make mistakes, it's good manners to let them know it in a nice way," said Angel.

No wonder her name is Angel, thought Amelia Bedelia.

"Right you are, Angel," said Mrs. Shauk. "Manners must be learned and practiced. They don't come naturally. We don't have our mouths open, hungry for good manners, like baby birds ready to gobble down a fat grub or juicy worm."

Amelia Bedelia loved how Mrs. Shauk made her lessons so memorable. She just wished she hadn't had such a big breakfast. Now all she could think about was worms!

Mrs. Shauk continued. "I was planning on starting a unit on weather, but I think our time would be better spent on manners instead. The weather will still be here after we learn how to best behave to one another. There is clearly no time like the present."

"A present?" asked Amelia Bedelia excitedly. "Who is it for?" Amelia Bedelia liked presents even better than picnics.

Mrs. Shauk smiled. "Well now that you mention it, there *could* be a very nice prize for everyone when we finish the unit. We're going to study manners. Table manners, meeting and greeting people, writing thank-you notes, having polite conversations, all kinds of manners. It is very important to have good manners. It shows respect to those around us and makes life more pleasant for everyone. If you all do a good job, when we are done we can celebrate with . . ."

The class was silent, not wanting to interrupt.

"An ice-cream party!" Mrs. Shauk finished.

Everyone cheered.

Mrs. Shauk smiled. "Let's start at the very beginning," she said. "With meeting and greeting people."

"My mom always tells me that it's important to make a good first impression," said Daisy.

"Your mother is right," said Mrs. Shauk. "How other people think about you and treat you begins with the impression you make from the very start. It is a foundation you can build upon."

"So, your first impression is way more important than your seventeenth impression," said Chip.

"Yes, most often that's the case," said

Mrs. Shauk. "In fact, meeting someone for the first time is a terrific way for us to begin our unit on manners. Let's practice."

"We're friends," said Amelia Bedelia. "We already know each other."

"Let's pretend we don't," said Mrs. Shauk. "If I met you for the first time, I would say, 'Hello, how do you do?'"

"How do I do what?" replied Amelia Bedelia.

"You don't have to do anything. Just smile," said Mrs. Shauk.

"This is easy," said Amelia Bedelia. She put on her best smile, one that she used for photos. This made the other kids giggle . . . which made Amelia Bedelia smile for real.

"Now what do I do?" asked Amelia Bedelia.

"Say hello, tell me how you are feeling, then ask, 'How are you doing?'"

"Oh, I'm fine," said Amelia Bedelia. "How am I doing?"

"Not you, *me*," said Mrs. Shauk. "I'm the one meeting you."

"That's too bad," said Amelia Bedelia. "I hope you do something more exciting today than just meet me!"

The class laughed.

Mrs. Shauk frowned. "Perhaps we should start again," she said.

Chapter 3

Meet and Greet

"Amelia Bedelia, can you come to the front of the room, please?" asked Mrs. Shauk.

"Yes, I can," said Amelia Bedelia. Even

though her desk was in the last row, her legs worked just fine. She sat up straight in her chair, still smiling as hard as she could.

"Amelia Bedelia," said Mrs. Shauk. Then she smiled, shook her head, and sighed. "Amelia Bedelia, would you walk to the front of the room, and stand next to me?"

"Sure," said Amelia Bedelia. She stood, and in a few seconds was standing next to Mrs. Shauk.

Mrs. Shauk reached out, took Amelia Bedelia's hand, and shook it. "Hello, my name is Mrs. Shauk. Nice to meet you," she said with a warm smile.

Amelia Bedelia snorted. "Now that's just silly," she said. "I know who you are. And you know who I am."

"This is a manners lesson," Mrs. Shauk

explained. "We're pretending that we are meeting for the first time."

"Oh, okay," said Amelia Bedelia. She stared at her teacher. "So what am I supposed to do now?"

"You could say, 'It's nice to meet you too,'" replied Mrs. Shauk.

Amelia Bedelia nodded. "It's nice to meet me too," she said.

Mrs. Shauk shook her head. "Not you, me."

"Not me?" asked Amelia Bedelia.

"No, not you," said Mrs. Shauk.

"And not you?" said Amelia Bedelia.

Mrs. Shauk took a deep breath. "You can't introduce me to myself," she said patiently.

Amelia Bedelia thought for a moment. "I can try," she said. "Mrs. Shauk, I'd like you to meet my teacher, Mrs. Shauk. Mrs. Shauk, this is Mrs.—"

"Enough!" said Mrs. Shauk.

Amelia Bedelia was surprised. "Mrs. Enough?" she asked. "When did you change your name to Mrs. Enough?"

BOOM!

The class froze, assuming that the *BOOM!* was Mrs. Shauk blowing her top. They quickly realized that the noise had come from Clay and Cliff, who were in a heap on the floor.

Mrs. Shauk walked over and looked

down at the two boys, her arms crossed. "What happened here?" she asked.

No answer.

"Clay was laughing so hard he started to slide out of his seat," Holly finally explained. "Cliff tried to grab him, but then both their desks flipped over and they fell onto the floor."

"Are you two okay?" asked Mrs. Shauk.

Still no answer.

And then Clay snorted. And Cliff

started laughing and could not stop. And Clay started laughing too. Soon, the whole class joined in.

Everyone but Mrs. Shauk, that is. She reached down and pulled Cliff and Clay to their feet.

"Go to the nurse's office and get checked out, please." Raising an eyebrow, she added, "It's right next to the principal's office."

Cliff and Clay stopped laughing. So did everyone else.

Amelia Bedelia kept her eyes on Mrs. Shauk. The Hawk was tapping her toe on the floor and shaking her head. "Since

when did manners get so confusing?"
Mrs. Shauk muttered.

"Maybe you should stop by the nurse's office too," Amelia Bedelia suggested.

"That's the best idea I've heard all day," Mrs. Shauk replied, sinking down in her chair. "Class dismissed for early recess."

Amelia Bedelia and her friends cheered.

On her way out of the classroom Amelia Bedelia paused in front of her teacher's desk. "It has been a pleasure, Mrs. . . . Enough."

Mrs. Shauk managed a weak smile. "Enough is enough," she said. "Get going!"

Chapter 4

Candy Is Dandy?

"This is going to be as easy as pie," said Pat. "I mean, how hard can it be? We just have to say 'please' and 'thank you' and 'how do you do?' and smile a lot, and we're all set." He glanced at his classmates, who were gathered around

their tree-stump table in the schoolyard.

"Pie?" said Amelia Bedelia. "I thought it was going to be an ice-cream party."

"It *is* going to be an ice-cream party," said Angel. "Though a pie party would be fun too. You could bake for us!"

Amelia Bedelia smiled. She was well known for her delicious lemon tarts. But her smile quickly turned into a frown. "I don't know if we're going to have *any* kind of party," she said worriedly. "Manners are so confusing."

Joy nodded. "And Mrs. Shauk said we'd be learning table manners too. Did you know that there are things like fish forks? And even oyster forks?"

oyster fork

fish fork

regular dinner fork

29

"I can't even remember to keep my elbows off the table," said Penny. "How am I going to remember which fork to use?"

"Sometimes I burp at the dinner table  and forget to say excuse me," Skip confessed.

"URP!" Clay  fake burped and gave Skip a high five.

Heather rolled her eyes.

Amelia Bedelia and her friends sat in silence. This manners stuff *was* complicated.

Pat sighed. "Maybe this isn't going to be as easy as I thought," he said.

Just then Joy stood up and pointed. "Hey, look!" she said. Across the yard

they could see a girl walking up to the school with her parents. A girl none of them had ever seen before. She wore a fancy outfit and had a pink streak in her hair that matched her boots perfectly.

"Maybe she'll be in our class," said Penny hopefully.

"No way," said Teddy, shaking his head. "She looks way older than us."

Just as Amelia Bedelia and the rest of the class got settled in their seats after recess, there was a knock at the door. Mrs. Shauk opened it. There stood Principal Hotchkiss and the new girl.

Amelia Bedelia knew it was probably not very good manners, but she couldn't help staring. The new girl was even cooler-looking up close. Her hair was held back with a butterfly headband. Her nails were florescent pink . . . except for her pinkie fingers, which were gold. Instead of an ordinary backpack, she had a plastic see-through tote bag slung over her shoulder. Inside it, Amelia Bedelia could see a big feathered pen, a sparkly notebook, a pair of star-shaped sunglasses, and a furry pencil case that looked like a panda bear's face.

Mrs. Shauk turned to the class.

"This is what I was going to tell you this morning, before . . . well. You remember. I am delighted to announce that we have a new student joining our classroom. She comes to us all the way from Chicago! And the timing couldn't be better." She turned to the new girl. "We just started our unit on manners. This is the perfect opportunity to practice our greetings."

Mrs. Shauk extended her hand to the new girl. "Pleased to meet you," she said. "My name is Mrs. Shauk."

The new girl smiled and shook Mrs. Shauk's hand. "It's a pleasure to meet you," she replied. "My name is Candy."

Candy! Amelia Bedelia didn't think she had ever heard a sweeter name.

After everyone in the class had introduced themselves to Candy, Mrs. Shauk pointed to the empty desk next to Amelia Bedelia. "You may sit there," she said.

"Why, thank you," said Candy. She hung her bag on the back of the chair and slid gracefully into the seat.

Mrs. Shauk beamed and said, "And may I say, Candy, your manners are impeccable."

Pat leaned over and high-fived

Daisy. "We're a shoo-in with Miss Manners in our class," he said.

Amelia Bedelia looked down at her high tops and then over at Candy's shiny pink boots. She had no idea what shoes had to do with anything. But she was feeling very positive about two things: 1. Candy's wonderful manners were going to help them win the ice-cream party, and 2. She was sure that she and the new girl were going to become very good friends.

Chapter 5

His Creases Have Creases

On Monday morning Amelia Bedelia unpacked her books, hung her backpack in the closet, put her lunch box into the bin, and got straight to work taking the chairs down from the top of the desks and sliding them into place. Her classroom job that month was Chair Patrol. It wasn't her favorite job. She would be glad when the month was over and she was assigned a new one. But she took it seriously just the same. She got to school early each day, sometimes even before Mrs. Shauk arrived.

Amelia Bedelia thought about the ice-cream party as she worked. Would Mrs. Shauk serve ice-cream cones? Would there also be ice-cream sundaes and banana splits? Would there be different toppings? And what about kids who preferred milk shakes and ice-cream sodas? It was a lot to think about.

A voice interrupted her thoughts. "Where's Mrs. Shauk?"

Amelia Bedelia looked up. It was Candy. Amelia Bedelia looked around.

Candy was right. Mrs. Shauk was nowhere to be seen. That was strange. It was almost time for school to begin.

Just then Dawn came racing into the classroom, out of breath. "You're never going to—"

"Hold your horses!" cried Wade. "You

know there's no running in the halls."

Amelia Bedelia slid the final chair into place and glanced at the job board. Yup, Wade was Hall Monitor. Then she stuck her head out of the classroom and looked right, then left . . . but all she saw were students.

"I was just in the main office, and you're never going to believe what I heard," Dawn continued. "Mrs. Shauk's mother is sick, and she took a leave of absence to take care of her."

"Whoa!" said Skip. "Isn't Mrs. Shauk too old to have a mother?"

"That's not very nice," said Angel.

"I heard it straight from the horse's mouth," Dawn insisted.

Amelia Bedelia was torn between feeling sad for Mrs. Shauk and her sick mom and feeling excited that there were horses at school.

"Where is the horse?" she asked. "In the main office?"

Dawn shook her head. "There is no horse. Just Mrs. Roman. She's the one who told me the news. Principal Hotchkiss is bringing a sub to our class right now!"

A sub! Amelia Bedelia had not been looking forward to the leftover pot roast and eggplant sandwich in her lunch box. A submarine sandwich would be a much tastier choice.

Amelia Bedelia and her friends sat at their desks and watched the door expectantly. But when the principal arrived, Amelia Bedelia was disappointed to see that Ms. Hotchkiss had not brought a submarine sandwich. Instead, she had brought along a sub *person*, a substitute for Mrs. Shauk. Standing beside her was a very tall man with very short hair.

"Class, Mrs. Shauk has been called away on urgent family business," Ms. Hotchkiss explained.

Amelia Bedelia looked at Dawn and wiggled her eyebrows.

"It is my pleasure to introduce you to Sergeant Strickland," continued Ms. Hotchkiss. "He was once a student

here at Oak Tree Elementary, just like all of you. He recently retired from the military, and luckily for us, he was available to be your substitute teacher until Mrs. Shauk returns. I am sure you will all be on your best behavior and make Oak Tree Elementary proud!" She nodded at the class and at the sergeant, and then left, closing the classroom door behind her.

Sergeant Strickland slowly surveyed the class, looking directly into the eyes of each student. He was not wearing a uniform, just a navy-blue blazer with gold buttons. His strong stance gave the impression of someone who could handle any situation. He gave the class a crisp salute. "At ease, people," he said. Amelia

Bedelia and her friends exhaled and leaned back in their chairs.

"Naturally, I expect outstanding behavior from each one of you while Mrs. Shauk is away," he said. "Roger that?"

Amelia Bedelia raised her hand. "Roger is in the other class," she explained.

"No Roger. Roger that," said the sergeant, glancing down at Mrs. Shauk's lesson book. "We will begin our march into manners with the most fundamental but most important skill of all, table manners."

Then Sergeant Strickland did what he would do every day that he taught them. He hung up his jacket, unbuttoned his cuffs, and rolled his sleeves up above his elbow. It was his signal that it was time to get to work.

Chip raised his hand. "Mrs. Shauk told us we're going to have an ice-cream party after we finish our unit on good manners," he said.

"Well, we'll see about that, son," said Sergeant Strickland. He sat down on the edge of Mrs. Shauk's desk. Amelia Bedelia stared at his crisp, ironed pants and polished shoes. It felt strange to have someone different in Mrs. Shauk's place, even though she knew it was only temporary.

"Basic table manners," Sergeant Strickland said. "List them."

"You should ask to be excused and not just leave the table after dinner," offered Rose.

"Affirmative," said the substitute.

Rose was confused, as was the rest of the class. "Does that mean I was right?" she asked.

"Affirmative," said Sergeant Strickland.

"Your napkin goes on your lap. Not tied around your neck," said Teddy.

Sergeant Strickland nodded again. "Affirmative. You are eating dinner, not chasing cattle rustlers," he said.

"And you definitely don't blow your nose into your napkin," said Penny.

"Or comb your hair or pick your teeth at the table. That's gross too," added Daisy.

"Talking about gross . . . you should never talk with your mouth full," said Clay. "I learned that the hard way. My parents had a dinner party. I took a big bite of food just as my dad's boss asked me what my favorite subject is in school. And instead of swallowing first, I said, 'Social studies,' and spit mashed potatoes all over his face."

The class erupted into laughter.

"Enough," said Sergeant Strickland. "We need to be serious."

"It was seriously disgusting," said Clay.

Sergeant Strickland pointed to Amelia Bedelia. "What if you are sitting at the dinner table and you want the brussels sprouts, but the bowl is not directly in front of you. What do you do?"

"Nothing," said Amelia Bedelia.

"Nothing?" said Sergeant Strickland.

"Nothing," said Amelia Bedelia. "I don't like brussels sprouts."

Sergeant Strickland shook his head. "Say they're string beans."

"They're string beans," said Amelia Bedelia. Then she frowned. "But you said they were brussels sprouts."

"Now they're string beans," said Sergeant Strickland. "What do you do?"

"Nothing," said Amelia Bedelia.

"Still nothing?" asked Sergeant Strickland.

"I don't like string beans either," Amelia Bedelia explained.

Sergeant Strickland raised his eyebrows. He pointed to Wade. "What would *you* do?"

Wade thought for a moment. "I would say excuse me and then reach for the bowl."

Sergeant Strickland shook his head. "Negative," he said.

"Um, I would say, 'Pardon my arm'?" Wade guessed.

"I think you mean 'Pardon my reach,'" said Sergeant Strickland.

Wade smiled. "Yup," he said.

"But that's still not correct," said Sergeant Strickland. He looked around the class. "Can anyone help us here?"

Candy spoke up. "It's bad manners to reach across the table. You should politely ask the person who is sitting closest to the bowl to pass it to you."

Sergeant Strickland nodded briskly. "Affirmative!" he said.

"We were taught manners at my old school in first grade," Candy said.

"Well, la-di-da," whispered Chip.

That morning they learned many new things:

1. Never point with a utensil.

2. Place your napkin to the left of the plate  when you are finished eating or when you get up from the table.

3. Never place used silverware on the table when you pause while eating; always rest it on your plate.

 4. Wait until everyone is served before starting your meal.

5. Don't blow on your food, no matter how hot it is.

6. Always pass the salt and pepper together, even if someone just asks for one of them.

7. If you drop a fork at a restaurant, don't pick it up. Ask for a new one.

Amelia Bedelia felt like her head was spinning. Table manners were turning out to be even more complicated than meeting and greeting manners. And that was saying a lot.

The day didn't get any easier. In art class while Amelia Bedelia and her friends were setting up, Wade tripped and spilled an entire jar of yellow paint. *SPLASH!* It ended up all over Amelia Bedelia and Candy.

SPLASH

Amelia Bedelia looked down at her splattered T-shirt. "We're finalists in a hot-dog-eating contest," she said to Candy with a grin.

But Candy scowled. "Maybe it's funny to you, but this is a designer sweater. And now it's ruined!"

And Amelia Bedelia had to eat the leftover pot roast and eggplant sandwich for lunch. That was the biggest disappointment of all.

Chapter 6

From the Outside In

After Amelia Bedelia got home and changed out of her paint-splattered clothes, she did her homework, then headed downstairs for dinner.

"Oh no," she said when she reached the dining room. "It's not your anniversary, is it?" The dining-room table was set with their finest china, cutlery;

53

and crystal, the stuff they only used for holidays and special occasions. There were cloth napkins, plus a fancy lace tablecloth and a floral centerpiece, and her mother had even polished her great-grandmother's silver candlesticks. Everything glowed in the candlelight. Amelia Bedelia did a quick count. There were eight utensils at each place setting. Eight!

"No, cupcake," said her mother. "That's not for another three months."

"Whew," said Amelia Bedelia. "Then is it—"

"Nope. It's not a holiday either," added her father. "When you told us you were learning table manners in school, we decided it was the perfect time to show you how a proper table is set.

"Please take your seats, ladies!"

Bread plate

Butter knife

Dessert spoon

Glass

Dessert fork

Napkin

Soup spoon

Salad fork

Dinner fork

Dinner plate

Dinner knife

Salad knife

Amelia Bedelia's father disappeared into the kitchen. Her mother picked up her cloth napkin, opened it, and placed it on her lap. Amelia Bedelia was relieved to see she didn't shake it out. She now knew that was bad manners.

"Are you ready to dig in?" her mother asked.

"No, but I am ready to eat," said Amelia Bedelia.

"Well, that's good news," said her father, returning to the dining room. "Because I come bearing the first course." He placed a bowl of soup on top of each dinner plate.

"Yum, tomato soup," said Amelia Bedelia. She stared

56

at the utensils and reached for the spoon above her plate. "This one?" she asked.

"That's the dessert spoon," explained her mother. "You need your soup spoon. It's to the right of your plate. The forks are always on the left and the knives and spoons are always on the right. Your soup spoon is at the far end." She picked hers up. "Here's the secret to navigating the cutlery. You work from the outside in. After every course, your utensils will be taken away. And the next one in line is what you will use next."

"That's easy to remember," said Amelia Bedelia. She was starting to feel a little bit hopeful. Maybe table manners wouldn't be so hard after all. She really really really wanted to be sure she and her friends earned their ice-cream party.

"Here's another trick," said her father. "I learned this after I mistakenly ate your grandfather's dinner roll the very first time I met him. It was tasty but embarrassing." He held up his hands and touched his index fingers to his thumbs, making the okay sign with each hand. "See how my 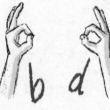 left hand forms a small *b* and the right one forms a small *d*?" Amelia Bedelia nodded.

"That's how you know that your bread plate is on your left and your drink is on your right. So you won't be eating your friend's bread. Or drinking from your friend's glass."

"Wow," said Amelia Bedelia. "What a great trick!"

While Amelia Bedelia and her parents ate their soup, Amelia  Bedelia made pleasant conversation as Sergeant Strickland had instructed.

". . . and that's why I don't think the new girl likes me very much," she concluded. "Or our school. And I was really hoping we would be friends."

"I'm sorry, sweetie," said her mother. "I guess Wade's paint spill really bent you out of shape."

Amelia Bedelia stood up and stretched her arms and legs. "No, I'm fine," she said. "Just disappointed." She sat back down.

"Well, how about a new course," said Amelia Bedelia's father. He cleared the soup bowls and served the salads.

"Now we use the salad fork and knife," said Amelia Bedelia's mother, picking up  the next two utensils in line, one from either side of her plate. Amelia Bedelia did the same.

"That's a lot of changes for you this week," said Amelia Bedelia's father. "A new classmate *and* a new teacher." He considered this for a moment. "But maybe Candy's having a hard time. Sounds like she might be feeling a bit like a fish out of water."

Amelia Bedelia shook her head. "There's nothing fishy about her."

"Maybe she doesn't feel like she fits in," her father said. "This move has probably been a very big adjustment for her. Maybe you could give her another chance."

"She makes it pretty hard," Amelia Bedelia said, spearing a tomato.

"I have an idea!" said Amelia Bedelia's mother. "Even though you may not feel like it on the inside, maybe you could try to be nice to her on the outside. It's another way of being polite."

Amelia Bedelia looked down at her plate and laughed. "Like the silverware? I should work from the outside in?"

61

Her mother nodded. "That's right. Just like the silverware! And if you do it enough times, you might even end up actually being friends. Remember when you were nervous before you spoke at my town council meeting, but you acted confident, which turned out to make you really *feel* confident too?"

Amelia Bedelia nodded. "That *did* work."

"That's right," said her father. "Sometimes you have to kill them with kindness!"

"Daddy!" said Amelia Bedelia.

Her father laughed. "Okay then. Just be really nice until she can't help but be nice right back."

Chapter 7

Volcanoes Are a Blast!

"Bye, Mom," said Amelia Bedelia as she headed out the door the next morning.

"Goodbye, babycakes," said her mother. "Hope you can turn over a new leaf today!"

That sounded like a strange thing to do. *But maybe it's for good luck,* Amelia Bedelia thought. So she did just that as she passed Mrs. Adams's maple tree on the way to school. She needed all the help she could get. She also decided she would try a new approach with Candy and Sergeant Strickland. She was going to be very positive and hope that her insides would catch up with her outside.

Amelia Bedelia was the very first student to arrive, as usual. She pushed open the door and spotted the sub sitting in Mrs. Shauk's chair, with his back to her.

"Good morning, Sergeant Strickland!" Amelia Bedelia sang out.

Startled, the sergeant spun around. A pink doughnut with rainbow

sprinkles stuck out of his mouth. He had a napkin covered with sprinkles tucked into his collar.

Amelia Bedelia stared at him for a second. This was not a sight you saw every day!

"I hope I didn't disturb your breakfast," she said politely. She picked up a chair and set it on the floor.

"Negative," he replied stiffly. But his cheeks were as pink as the frosting on his doughnut.

When Candy arrived, Amelia Bedelia kept a close eye on her, waiting for an opportunity to be kind.

"Why do you keep staring at me?"

Candy finally asked.

Amelia Bedelia searched for a compliment. "Your hair is looking very . . . clean today! You did a good job washing out the yellow paint."

Candy looked puzzled and rolled her eyes. "Um, thank you?" she said. She gave Amelia Bedelia an odd look and then ignored her the whole rest of the class.

At recess, Amelia Bedelia spotted Candy sitting by herself on the swings. Was it her imagination, or did Candy look a little bit lonely? Amelia Bedelia headed across the playground, determined to be nice to her.

"Amelia Bedelia!" Skip shouted. "Over here!"

Amelia Bedelia spun around. Clay was frantically waving at her from the tree stump table where the rest of her classmates were gathered. Amelia Bedelia gave one last glance at Candy, then headed over to her friends.

"We're having an emergency meeting," said Pat. "Can someone please find out when Mrs. Shauk is coming back? I can't

take much more of Sergeant Strickland."

"What are *you* complaining about?" said Wade. "He made me do ten push-ups when I couldn't identify the noun in a sentence. I was like, 'Dude, it's language arts, not gym class!'"

"And I'm not sure about that new girl either," added Rose. "I don't think she likes us very much."

"Maybe we should try destroying them both with friendliness," Amelia Bedelia said. She frowned. That didn't sound right. She tried again. "I mean, let's be extra nice and maybe they'll be nice back."

Heather sighed. "I don't know about that. He's the worst

substitute Oak Tree Elementary has ever had. He never smiles."

"And he doesn't let us have any fun," said Holly. "He's the worst substitute in the history of substitute teachers!"

"Wow," said Amelia Bedelia. "That would make him really really bad."

"He is!" exclaimed Dawn. "He's a total disaster!"

"A major catastrophe!" said Cliff.

Clay punched Cliff in the arm. "That's it! That's his nickname. Major Catastrophe!"

Tweet! Sergeant Strickland blew his whistle. Recess was definitely over.

Tweeet!

69

"Well, at least he doesn't make us run laps," Angel said softly as they lined up in size order, shortest to tallest.

Teddy glanced around. "Shhhh, don't give him any ideas!"

That afternoon in science class, Amelia Bedelia grabbed a seat right next to Candy.

Ms. Garcia grinned at the class. "Today we are going to learn about chemical reactions," she said. "Specifically, acid-base reactions."

Candy yawned. "I hope it's not the erupting volcano experiment," she muttered. "At my school we did that in first grade."

Although Amelia Bedelia

really wanted to be kind to her, Candy wasn't making it very easy. She made a lot of comments about how things were better at her old school. The classes were more interesting. The cafeteria food was better. And the after-school clubs rocked.

Actually, Amelia Bedelia really hoped that they *would* be making volcanos in class. That sounded like her kind of fun.

"In other words, we'll be building volcanos and making them erupt!" announced Mrs. Garcia.

The class cheered. Candy sighed and slumped down in her chair.

"Now, everyone grab a partner. You'll need to get the following materials in the back of the room: goggles, an empty

goggles

water bottle

clay

food
coloring

metal
tray

BakingSoda

recyclable water bottle, clay, a metal
tray, red food coloring, vinegar,
dish soap, baking soda,
and your lab instructions."

dish
soap

vinegar

baking
soda

Amelia Bedelia turned to Candy and
grabbed her arm. "Partners?" she asked.

Candy shrugged. "Fine, sure,
why not?" she replied.

lab
instructions

How to
make a
Volcano

LAB INSTRUCTIONS

1. Put a tablespoon of baking soda into
the water bottle.

2. Use the clay to build a volcano
around the water bottle. Place the
volcano on the metal tray.

3. Add a few drops of red food coloring
to the mouth of the volcano, to make it

72

look like lava, plus a drop or two of dish soap, to make it extra bubbly.

4. Put on your goggles and pour a quarter cup of vinegar into the volcano. When the baking soda (the base) and the vinegar (the acid) combine, they will produce carbon dioxide gas that looks just like an erupting volcano!

Amelia Bedelia got the lab instructions and the goggles, water bottle, and clay. Candy picked up the food coloring, vinegar, dish soap, and baking soda. They started building their volcano, smoothing brown and green clay around the bottle.

They stepped back to check their work.

"It looks great!" said Amelia Bedelia.

Candy nodded. "It does look pretty good," she said.

Candy added three drops of red food coloring and two drops of dish soap into the bottle. The two girls put on their goggles. Amelia Bedelia was so excited

she forgot to measure the vinegar and poured it in, right out of the bottle.

"Wait!" cried Candy.

"Isn't that too much vin—"

Whoosh! The volcano erupted.

"Great chemical reaction!" said Ms. Garcia, coming over to see.

The entire class watched as the bubbly pink "lava"

flowed down the sides of the volcano.

"Cool!" said Wade.

"Awesome!" said Penny.

"I think you forgot something," said Joy. "Your metal tray!"

They all watched helplessly as the pink liquid lava oozed off the table . . .

. . . and directly onto Candy's yellow ballerina flats. She gasped. Ms. Garcia hurried off to get paper towels.

"I can't look," Candy said. "Is it bad?"

Amelia Bedelia looked at Candy's feet. "Not bad at all," she said. "As long as you like tie-dye, that is."

"Amelia Bedelia!" Candy yelled. "You ruined my new shoes!"

Dawn came over and put her arm around Amelia Bedelia. "You don't need to bite her head off!" she told Candy.

Amelia Bedelia looked at Candy, then looked back at Dawn. "I don't think she will," she said. "She's just mad at me."

"Well, you shouldn't talk to my friend that way," Dawn told Candy. "It was an accident."

❀❀❀

On her way home, Amelia Bedelia thought about the two things she had learned that day:

Acids and bases mixed together make chemical reactions. And sometimes a mess.

And even though Candy had the best manners in class, Amelia Bedelia was starting to think that maybe she wasn't all that nice.

Chapter 8

At an Escargot's Pace

Amelia Bedelia sat down in her seat and smoothed her flowered skirt. She looked around the classroom. Everyone was in their fanciest clothes. Joy had on a long dress with puffy sleeves and shoes with little heels. Holly wore a bright red dress, a charm bracelet, and a necklace with a gold locket. Most of the boys wore button-down shirts and dress pants. Pat even had a bow tie and vest. Candy walked in wearing a sleek jumpsuit, her hair in a bun on top of her head.

"She might not be the friendliest person, but she really has an eye for fashion," said Dawn.

"Just one?" asked Amelia Bedelia.

"Just one what?" asked Dawn. She was wearing a silky blue dress and matching shoes with big bows on them.

"Just one eye?" said Amelia Bedelia.

Dawn raised her eyebrows. "No, I'm pretty sure she has two," she said. "At least I hope so!"

The class had been studying their table manners for weeks, and now it was time to put them to the test. They were taking a field trip to the fanciest restaurant in town. It was called L'Escargot, and they had learned the name was French for "snail" and that was also the restaurant's specialty. Everyone in town knew that L'Escargot was *the* place to go to celebrate special occasions. Amelia Bedelia had been there just once before, for her grandmother's birthday. She had passed on the snails.

Sergeant Strickland looked around the room. "Everyone is dressed to the nines!" he said. He wore a crisp pressed white shirt, blue pants, a tie, and his usual navy-blue jacket.

"I think we're dressed to the tens!" said Amelia Bedelia.

"Affirmative!" said Sergeant Strickland.

The class lined up, shortest to tallest, and headed out of the classroom. Mrs. Roman looked up from her desk as they trooped by the main office. "Bon appétit!" she called out.

"Now remember to say please and thank you," Sergeant

Strickland reminded them along the way. "And no chewing with your mouth open."

When they arrived at L'Escargot, a man in a tuxedo came outside to greet them. While he chatted with Sergeant Strickland (in French, no less), Amelia Bedelia and her friends stared at the restaurant. It had a red sidewalk awning, gleaming glass windows, and the name L'ESCARGOT

written on the main window in gold script.

"Hey, why did the snail paint the letter S on his new car?" Clay asked.

"Beats me," said Cliff. "Why?"

"So everyone would say, 'Look at that S car go!'" Clay answered.

"I don't get it," said Chip.

"Are you telling me you don't know what escargot is?" asked Candy. "It's snails. In a butter-and-garlic sauce."

"No way," said Wade. "You're making that up," He suddenly looked nervous.

"Way," said Candy.

"The young lady is correct," said the man in the tuxedo. "Hello, ladies and gentlemen. My name is Pierre, and I am the maître d'. Have you had escargot before?" he asked Candy.

Candy bit her lip and paused for a moment.

"Of course," she finally said. "I adore that dish."

"Wow," said Wade. "I'll believe it when I see it!"

Sergeant Strickland held the door open, and Amelia Bedelia and her friends filed into the hushed interior of the

restaurant, their dress-up shoes sinking into the soft carpet. The only sounds were the murmur of quiet voices and the soft clinking of utensils against the fine china. Amelia Bedelia took it all in, the gold and crystal chandeliers, the uniformed waiters, the bright white tablecloths, and the rich red velvet curtains.

Pierre led them past several well-dressed diners to a large table set with gleaming china and silverware. Amelia Bedelia noticed that no one seemed to want to sit next to Candy, so she was polite on the outside and slipped into the seat next to her.

She looked around at the serious faces of her classmates. It was one thing to practice good manners in the classroom. She looked down at the array of silverware and immediately forgot everything she had learned. Was she supposed to work from the inside out or the outside in? And was it top to bottom, side to side, and bottom to top? Which one was her bread plate? Which glass was she supposed to drink out of? From the expressions on her friends' faces, she could tell that they were feeling a bit worried too.

Sergeant Strickland picked up his napkin, unfolded it, and placed it on his lap. After a moment, so did everyone else. "No need to be nervous," he told them. "You know what to do. Just mind your manners and everything will be fine."

Pierre explained to the students that they would be enjoying four courses:

onion soup, a mixed green salad, chicken cordon bleu, and éclairs for dessert.

"Éclairs!" said Sergeant Strickland. "My favorite."

éclair

A woman appeared, dressed in white and wearing a tall hat. She held a small dish in her hands. "Bonjour, students," she said. "My name is Suzette, and I

am the head chef. I wanted to welcome you to our restaurant. And I hear we have an escargot fan at the table. Where is she?"

Everyone pointed at Candy. Was it Amelia Bedelia's imagination, or did their new student suddenly look very pale?

"We only have one more serving of

escargot left, so I saved it for you," Chef Suzette  said. She smiled and placed the snails in front of Candy, along with a pair of tongs and a small fork. Candy stared at the little snails still in their shells. She looked as though she might be about to cry.

"Go on," said Dawn. "I've never seen anyone eat snails before."

"I . . . I . . . ," stammered Candy.

"Whoa," said Wade. "Are you really going to eat those things?"

"I . . . I . . . ," stammered Candy.

"That is so gross," said Clay. "I dare you."

Candy, her face pale, looked at Amelia Bedelia in desperation.

Amelia Bedelia looked back. Then she lunged for her bread plate. Her arm knocked into Candy's water glass, dumping enough water to drown the escargot.

"Oh no, c'est dommage!" cried Chef Suzette, scooping up the slurpy dish. "I'm so sorry, but you cannot eat soggy escargot—the flavor is ruined!"

"Remember, class, we never reach for things, we ask for them to be passed to us," scolded Sergeant Strickland.

"Yeah, thanks for nothing, Amelia Bedelia," said Candy. "I didn't even get to have one."

"My apologies," said Amelia Bedelia. Just then she noticed that Skip, who sat on her other side, was reaching for her drink.

"Psst!" she said. "Don't you know about the b's and d's?"

Skip looked puzzled. "Is that like minding my p's and q's?" he asked.

"Your peas and what?" asked Amelia Bedelia. She shook her head. "No, your b's and d's." She did the okay sign with both hands. "The little *b* is for your bread plate and the little *d* is for your drink," she explained.

Skip grinned. "That makes it so easy!"

he said. He passed the trick on to Wade, who was sitting on his other side. In no time, everyone in the entire class was confidently eating the bread and drinking the water that belonged to them.

Their first course, onion soup, was served. A couple of

kids struggled with the long sticky strands of melted cheese, and Chip had to be reminded to wipe his chin.

The salad course was easier, but there were still a few manners mistakes. Skip didn't pass the salt and pepper together, and Heather left the table to go to the bathroom and forgot about her napkin. She was halfway across the room when it fell off her skirt and landed on the floor. A waiter quickly whisked it away, got a new one and placed it on her chair, and all was fine.

And everyone loved the chicken cordon bleu, which turned out to be chicken stuffed with ham and cheese and quite delicious.

Amelia Bedelia realized she was getting full. Since she wanted to save room for dessert, she placed her knife and fork in the "I'm done" position she had learned. Since she had only

"I am finished"

finished half her entrée, she was hoping she could take it home with her.

"May I put your food in a doggie bag, so you can take it home?" the waiter asked when he came to clear her plate.

"Oh no, I'd like to eat it myself," she said, wondering how the waiter knew she had a dog. "May I have it in a person bag instead?"

"But of course," said the waiter with a smile.

Sergeant Strickland seemed to relax a bit while the dishes were cleared. He nodded at the class as the waiters swept up the crumbs, and refilled the water glasses. The dessert course was next.

"Mmmmm," said Sergeant Strickland, rubbing his hands together. "It's the moment we've been waiting for!"

Wade picked up his dessert fork in anticipation. But it slipped through his fingers and fell to the floor. He forgot that he was supposed to leave it there and ask the waiter for another one, and he ducked under the table to pick it up.

As the waiter approached the table with a huge silver tray loaded with éclairs, Wade popped up, clutching his fork. "Found it!" he announced.

THUMP! His head hit the bottom of the platter, launching the chocolate-covered

éclairs into the air. The pastries went flying every which way.

"Oh non!" cried one of the waiters.

Amelia Bedelia and her friends watched as the éclairs splattered on the floor, the table, every nearby surface. Amelia Bedelia

winced as an éclair hit the oil painting on the wall behind her, leaving a trail of chocolate across the woodland scene.

As the waiters picked the pastries up off the floor, Pierre hurried over, wringing his hands. "I am so sorry," he said. "But we

have no more éclairs. Perhaps a nice fruit plate?"

Chip looked down and realized he had a squashed éclair on his lap. He held it up, pastry cream dripping between his fingers. "Look!" he said to Sergeant Strickland. "I saved you one!"

Sergeant Strickland just groaned and shook his head.

"And that is what you call a major catastrophe," said Cliff. "For Major Catastrophe!"

On the walk back to school Clay couldn't resist telling one more snail joke. "Why don't they serve escargot at hot-dog stands?" he asked.

"I don't know," said Dawn. "Why don't they serve escargot at hot-dog stands?"

"Because they only serve fast food!" Clay replied.

The class laughed. Amelia Bedelia stole a glance at Sergeant Strickland. She wasn't sure, but she thought she might have seen a tiny smile tugging on the corners of his mouth.

But he stared straight ahead and said "Ten-*hut*! Forward march!"

And that was the end of that.

Chapter 9

Small Talk, Big Results

The next day at school, everyone said "please" and "thank you" and "may I" and "don't mind if I do" to each other. They held doors open, and no one called out in class or spoke out of turn. They were hoping that if they were on their very best behavior, Sergeant Strickland would forget about yesterday's disaster and still let them have the ice-cream party.

After a lesson on how to write thank-you notes, Amelia Bedelia and her friends wrote to the staff of L'Escargot. Everyone concentrated very hard, wanting to write the most polite notes they could, in their very best handwriting.

To everyone at L'Escargot,
Thank you for treating us to lunch. I loved ♡ your food very much. It was even more delicious for dinner last night. I hope you were able to get the chocolate sauce off your fancy painting.
Best wishes,
Amelia Bedelia

Dear Pierre, Suzette, and the waitstaff,
We had a lovely time at your restaurant yesterday. Thank you for your hospitality. And thanks also for making escargot especially for me, even though I didn't get any. I'm sure they were quite delicious.
Sincerely,
Candy

To the staff of
L'Escargot,
I loved the French onion
soup, the salad, and the
Chicken Cordon Bleu. I'm
sure I would have also loved
the eclairs, but I knocked
them all over the floor. I am
very sorry about that.
With regrets,
Wade

Dear L'Escargot,
Your restaurant rocks!
We really had a
great time yesterday.
And your food is very
tasty. Thank you for
being so generous.
From, Clay

P.S. Here's a joke for you.
What is a snail's favorite
article of clothing?
Escargot Pants!

"That was a good effort, people," said
Sergeant Strickland.

The class looked at him expectantly, hoping he would add, "So good that the ice-cream party is definitely on!" But he did not.

"This afternoon we're going to learn how to make polite conversation," Sergeant Strickland announced when they all returned to the classroom after lunch.

Amelia Bedelia raised her hand. "I have a question. What's the best way to politely tell someone he has chocolate on their teeth?"

"Excellent question, Amelia Bedelia!" said Sergeant Strickland. "If it's just the two of you, you should say, 'You have something in your teeth.' But if you're in a group and you don't want to embarrass the person, it's best to point to your teeth and hope they get the idea."

Amelia Bedelia pointed to her teeth.

Sergeant Strickland nodded.

"Yes, just like that," he said.

Amelia Bedelia pointed to her teeth again.

"Correct," he said. Then a look of realization crossed his face. "Oh! Are you telling me that *I* have chocolate on my teeth?" He covered his mouth with his hand.

"Affirmative," said Amelia Bedelia.

Candy shook her head at Amelia Bedelia, as if to say, "What

were you thinking?" The rest of the class looked worried. Had Amelia Bedelia embarrassed Sergeant Strickland and made him mad?

But once he had taken care of the problem, Sergeant Strickland turned to the class. "It is always good manners to help someone out of an embarrassing situation," he said. He cleared his throat. "Especially when they are unaware of it."

He then divided everyone into groups of two. Each pair would stand in front of the class and have a polite conversation while everyone else listened.

"In a polite conversation you can ask questions, as long as they are respectful," explained Sergeant Strickland. "You should express interest in what the other person is talking about. You can share interesting stories and offer advice."

Clay and Cliff went first.

"Why don't you talk about your favorite subject at school?" Sergeant Strickland suggested.

Clay started. "Hey, Cliff, what is your favorite subject in school?" he asked.

"Thanks for asking, Clay," said Cliff. "I enjoy math. It feels like a game to me. I like figuring out the answers."

"How interesting," said Clay.

"Great job, guys," said Sergeant Strickland.

"Hey, Cliff, do you know why six is afraid of seven?" Clay asked.

"Oh no," said Sergeant Strickland.

"I'm afraid I don't, Clay," said Cliff. "Why is six afraid of seven?"

"Because seven ate nine," said Clay.

The class burst into laughter.

"Next!" said Sergeant Strickland.

Angel and Heather went to the front of the room.

"Please discuss your hobbies," said

Sergeant Strickland. "Heather, you first."

Heather smiled. "Hi, Angel. I actually have ten different hobbies, and I'd love to tell you all about them. The first is arts and crafts. I like doing tie-dye, embroidering, crocheting, painting, drawing, and sculpting. But not knitting. My grandma tried to teach me, but I just didn't get it. I also enjoy reading. I would say that I read a book a week. I

really like nonfiction books. I just finished a book about Nellie Bly, and it was really fascinating. Did you know that she went around the world in seventy-two days? I love playing card games, especially go fish and crazy eights." She paused for a minute and counted on her fingers. "That's three. I also enjoy roller skating and . . ."

"Very informative," said Sergeant Strickland. "But don't forget that when you have a polite conversation, you take turns talking. Why don't you tell us about your hobbies, Angel?"

"I like animals," said Angel quietly.

"Oh, me too!" said Heather. "Cats are my favorite. But I also like dogs and hamsters and gerbils. And I also like—"

"All righty then," interrupted Sergeant Strickland. He checked his watch. "We have time for one more conversation. Let's see, how about Amelia Bedelia and

Candy? Why don't you two talk about your plans for the weekend? Amelia Bedelia, you go first."

Amelia Bedelia smiled at Candy. "I'm excited for this weekend," she said. "I'm going to have a sleepover with a friend of mine from camp, and then I'm going to take my dog, Finally, to the dog park and go on a bike ride with my parents."

"That sounds like fun," said Candy. "What kind of dog is Finally?"

Amelia Bedelia shrugged. "My dad says we should have called her Heinz. Because she's fifty-seven varieties."

"That's funny," said Candy.

"Do you like dogs?" asked Amelia Bedelia.

"I do," said Candy. "But we couldn't get one when we lived in Chicago because our apartment building didn't allow them."

"Very good conversing," said Sergeant Strickland. "I like the back-and-forth. Class, I hope you are paying attention."

"What are you doing this weekend?" Amelia Bedelia asked.

"My mom and I are going shopping to decorate my new bedroom," Candy replied.

"That sounds great. You should go to this store called Rosie's Room," said Amelia Bedelia. "They have really nice pillows and rugs and stuff."

Candy shrugged. "I'm sure it won't be as nice as the stores in Chicago," she said.

Amelia Bedelia felt bad for Candy. She clearly missed her old home very much. Amelia Bedelia decided to offer some advice. "You really miss Chicago. Why don't you ask your parents if you can move back?" she said.

"Amelia Bedelia!" said Sergeant

Strickland. "That is not very polite!"

Amelia Bedelia was confused. "I was just offering helpful advice, like you said."

"I am very disappointed," said Sergeant Strickland. "You need to apologize."

Amelia Bedelia took a deep breath. "Sorry if my advice upset you," she said, looking at the floor.

"Amelia Bedelia, do you really mean that? It sounds like you are only saying the words because I asked you to." Sergeant Strickland turned to the class. "Do you think that was a proper apology?"

Dawn shrugged. "Sounded good to me," she said. The rest of the class nodded in agreement.

Sergeant Strickland shook his head in disbelief. "That apology is utterly inadequate. I clearly have not been doing my job very well. That's it. The ice-cream party is officially canceled."

"But Major Catastrophe—I mean, Sergeant Strickland . . . ," began Amelia Bedelia.

Her friends couldn't help it. They burst out laughing.

Sergeant Strickland's face turned bright red. "Not another word. And that's an order."

Chapter 10

Killed by Kindness

Amelia Bedelia was very busy that weekend and didn't have a lot of time to think about what had happened at school. Every time her mind turned to it, she pushed it away. But by Sunday evening, she started to worry. Was Candy really upset? Was the whole class mad at her for ruining the ice-cream party? She sat at the dinner table and sighed.

"Amelia Bedelia, why do you look so blue?" her mother asked.

Amelia Bedelia looked down at her arms. "I do? No, I don't." She sighed again. "I *am* feeling a little sad, though." She explained what had happened at school. "And now Candy thinks I'm mean and now we're never going to have the ice-cream party."

Amelia Bedelia's mother shook her head. "I know that you were trying to be helpful," she said. "And I'm so sorry you had that misunderstanding." She looked

over at Amelia Bedelia's father. "Daddy and I have noticed that your manners really have been improving since you started learning about manners at school. You can fix this easily. You just have to apologize—sincerely—to Candy."

"Even though she's not so nice and I've been trying so hard?" Amelia Bedelia asked.

Her father nodded. "Two wrongs don't make a right," he said.

"I know," said Amelia Bedelia. "Two wrongs make two wrongs. Everybody knows that."

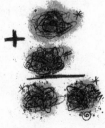

On Monday morning, Amelia Bedelia walked slowly to school. She knew she was going to be late, but she wanted to postpone apologizing to Candy for as long as possible. She lowered her head and concentrated on the sidewalk. What would she say? She still had no idea.

THUMP!

She had crashed into someone. She looked up. It was Candy.

"Hello, Amelia Bedelia," Candy said coldly. "Still think I should move back to Chicago?"

Amelia Bedelia got right to the point. "I'm sorry," she said. "I didn't mean to be rude. I was just wondering why you live here if you miss Chicago so much. I mean, I really love living here and I wouldn't want to live anywhere else."

"Well, I didn't have a choice," Candy said. "My mom got a new job and we had to move." She bit her lip. "I miss my friends and my school. It's hard being the new girl. I just wanted everyone to like me the way that they like you"

She stopped and turned to Amelia Bedelia. "Let's turn over a new leaf," she said.

"I did that already," said Amelia Bedelia. "But let's be friends."

"Do you think if we tell Sergeant Strickland we made up, he'll let us have the ice-cream party?" asked Candy.

Amelia Bedelia thought for a moment. "I think we might have to do something special to convince him. Maybe a big apology in class."

Candy smiled. "I have an idea," she said. She whispered it to Amelia Bedelia.

"I love it!" cried Amelia Bedelia. She whispered a few suggestions to Candy.

"That's perfect!" said Candy.

Amelia Bedelia grabbed

Candy's hand and squeezed it.

Candy squeezed back, but then looked down at the ground. "Um, if we're going to be friends, I have a confession to make," she said. "I . . . I fibbed. I never had escargot before. I was just showing off to look cool in front of the class. And I totally freaked out when they served them to me. I was so happy when you knocked over the glass of water on them."

Amelia Bedelia smiled. "I know," she said. "That's why I did it."

Chapter 11

Say You're Sorry

"So how was your weekend, sir?" Wade asked Sergeant Strickland first thing that morning. Before Sergeant Strickland had a chance to answer, Wade pressed  on. "Did you happen to change your mind about the ice-cream party?"

"Negative." Sergeant

Strickland shook his head. "My decision is final."

The entire class groaned with disappointment. Amelia Bedelia looked over at Candy and nodded encouragingly. Candy raised her hand.

"Yes?" Sergeant Strickland said.

"Amelia Bedelia and I came up with a plan on the way to school this morning. It will show that we really have been paying attention to you. We think it might change your mind about the party," she said.

"I'm all ears," said Sergeant Strickland, sitting on the corner of Mrs. Shauk's desk.

Amelia Bedelia leaned forward and took a look. "Oh,

don't worry, they're not that big," she said.

Candy held up several pieces of folded paper.

"It's called the I'm Sorry Game," said Amelia Bedelia. "We wrote different rude behaviors on these pieces of paper. Two kids will pick one and act out the scene for the class, like charades. We'll all guess what's wrong. And then we'll come up with a proper apology."

Cliff and Clay wanted to go first. Amelia Bedelia handed them a slip of paper.

Sneezing while not covering your mouth.

Cliff stood across from Clay, breathing in heavily, as if he was just about to sneeze. Then he snapped his head forward, his mouth open. Clay recoiled in disgust.

"I've got it!" said Holly. "The bad behavior is that Cliff threw up all over Clay. Gross!"

Skip raised his hand. "And Cliff should say, 'I apologize for barfing all over your shoes.'"

The class roared with laughter. But a quick glance at Sergeant Strickland quieted them all down.

Joy raised her hand. "I think that maybe Cliff sneezed without covering his mouth."

"Affirmative!" said Amelia Bedelia. "And what's the right apology?"

"Cliff should say, 'I'm sorry for sneezing on you.' And next time he should do this." She bent her arm and fake sneezed into the crook of her elbow. "The Dracula!"

Everyone immediately began fake sneezing into their elbows. They all loved the Dracula.

After the class had acted out breaking a friend's toy, not holding the door open for someone, and wiping your nose on your sleeve, it was Heather and Holly's turn.

Holly handed Heather something. Heather smiled and opened it. Then her face fell. Holly watched, looking very disappointed.

Pat guessed first. "I know! Your mom packed you smelly sardines for lunch. You are super disappointed about it. You wanted roast beef instead."

Penny poked him. "That was you," she reminded him. "I remember . . . I was sitting next to you!"

Pat laughed. "You're right!"

Penny spoke up. "I think that Holly gave Heather a gift and Heather didn't like it very much. Heather should have smiled and said, 'Thank you very much.' Because it's the thought that counts."

"Well put," said Sergeant Strickland.

"We have one more," said Amelia

Bedelia. "Candy and I will act it out."

She and Candy sat at their desks, fake talking to each other. Then Amelia Bedelia said something that made Candy silently gasp and put her hand to her mouth.

The class was quiet. Finally Angel spoke up. "I think that Amelia Bedelia said something that hurt Candy's feelings."

Amelia Bedelia nodded. "And my apology should be, 'I'm very sorry, Candy. I thought I was being helpful, but now I realize it was rude and I hurt your feelings. We're really glad to have you here at Oak Tree Elementary, and we really hope you stay.'"

"Thank you," said Candy. "And I just

want to say that I'm really happy to be here. I know I haven't been so easy to get along with, and I hope to change that and become friends with all of you!"

"Us too!" said Daisy.

Amelia Bedelia and her friends cheered.

"Class, I am officially impressed!" said Sergeant Strickland.

"So does that mean we're going to have the party?" asked Wade.

Everyone leaned forward in great anticipation.

But all Sergeant Strickland would say was, "We'll cross that bridge when we come to it."

Chapter 12

I Scream, You Scream

Amelia Bedelia arrived at school bright and early Tuesday morning and pushed open the classroom door. And there, to her great surprise and delight, stood Mrs. Shauk, writing on the whiteboard.

"You're back!" cried Amelia Bedelia. "How's

your family business?"

Mrs. Shauk smiled. "My mother is feeling much better. Thank you for asking." She smiled. "You are a sight for sore eyes!"

"Oh no, did you catch sore eyes from your mother?" asked Amelia Bedelia. "I hope you feel better soon."

"Thank you, Amelia Bedelia," said Mrs. Shauk, looking slightly confused.

As the students filed into the classroom, they broke into smiles as soon as they saw Mrs. Shauk. "Hey, hey, hey—the Hawk has landed!" Cliff shouted.

"Whoo-hoo!" said Dawn.

After the class had settled down, Mrs. Shauk said, "So I received a full report, literally, from my substitute." She held up a thick stack of paper. "He said that you had some ups and downs. And that there was a real breach of etiquette last week."

"Uh-oh," muttered Clay.

"But he also said that you managed to fix it and rally together as a class. And that he was proud of your growth. The ice-cream party is on, today after lunch! You pulled it off!"

"Pulled what off?" Amelia Bedelia asked Candy.

"Who cares?" said

Candy. "We're having an ice-cream party!"

Amelia Bedelia waited for her to say something about how the ice cream in Chicago was much better than anything they'd be able to get at Oak Tree Elementary. But Candy just looked happy.

"I told you this ice-cream party was in the bag," said Pat.

"I hope we have cones too!" said Amelia Bedelia.

The morning zoomed by. Soon it was time for recess. As the class walked down the hallway on their way outside, Amelia Bedelia had a sudden idea. She darted into the

main office for a moment. When she was done, she headed to the stump table. She smiled. She couldn't wait for the party.

When Amelia Bedelia and her friends returned from lunch, they discovered that all their desks had been pushed together. There were huge tubs of ice cream in familiar flavors like chocolate, vanilla, and strawberry, and in unexpected flavors such as blueberry cheesecake, avocado, and maple ripple. There was whipped cream, every kind of fruit from bananas to pineapple, plus toppings like hot fudge, caramel, strawberry sauce, sprinkles, walnuts, gummy bears, and cherries. There was root beer for root beer floats and chocolate soda for ice cream sodas. And even a blender for making milkshakes.

"We've got everything but the kitchen sink!" said Mrs. Shauk.

"Thank goodness," said Amelia Bedelia. She joined Candy at the table and started making herself a banana split.

"Oops!" Candy dropped a blob of hot fudge on her shirt.

"Oh no," said Amelia Bedelia.

"Don't worry," said Candy. "I learned my lesson. From now on I only wear clothes to school that I don't mind getting dirty. I don't want to miss out on any fun."

"So what did you and your friends do for fun in your old neighborhood, Candy?" asked Wade.

Candy smiled. "I'd rather hear about my *new* town. Like, what do you guys like to do on weekends?"

"Art classes at the Upcycling Art Studio," said Daisy.

"I volunteer at the animal shelter too," said Amelia Bedelia.

As Clay and Cliff launched into an explanation of the best bike paths in town, Mrs. Shauk, who had just taken a big spoonful of her sundae, couldn't help but blurt out, "Great polite conversation, class!"

Amelia Bedelia stared at her teacher. "Mind your manners, Mrs. Shauk!" she said. "You know you are not supposed to talk with your mouth full!"

The class froze and the room fell silent. Everyone stared at Amelia Bedelia. Then they stared at Mrs. Shauk. Was Mrs. Shauk going to get angry?

But she just wiped her mouth with a napkin and smiled. "Thank you, Amelia Bedelia. We could all use a reminder from time to time."

KNOCK! KNOCK!

Amelia Bedelia dashed over to open the door, with Mrs. Shauk on her heels. And there stood their substitute teacher. "Mrs. Shauk, allow me to introduce Sergeant Strickland," said

Amelia Bedelia. "I hope it's okay that I invited him to our ice-cream party."

"Of course it is, Amelia Bedelia!" said Mrs. Shauk. "Sergeant Strickland, it is lovely to meet you. Thank you so much for taking care of my class during my absence."

"It was my pleasure," said Sergeant Strickland.

"Are you sure?" asked Amelia Bedelia.

He nodded. "I am."

"Help yourself," said Mrs. Shauk, pointing to the ice-cream table.

"Don't mind if I do," said Sergeant Strickland.

"Why, Amelia Bedelia," said Mrs. Shauk.

"What a lovely idea to invite Sergeant Strickland. I see you really did learn how to mind your manners while I was away."

"Well, he did a great job teaching us," explained Amelia Bedelia. "Plus, I knew he'd hate to miss it."

Sergeant Strickland joined them, balancing a double-dip cone of chocolate chip and rocky road.

"Thanks for inviting me," said Sergeant Strickland. "Especially since I am a Major Catastrophe."

Amelia Bedelia blushed. "Actually," she said, "we are all so grateful to you for teaching us manners that we promoted you . . . from Major Catastrophe to General Nuisance."

"Amelia Bedelia, mind your manners!" said Mrs. Shauk.

Sergeant Strickland turned and saluted the class. Amelia Bedelia and her friends saluted him back. And for the first time since they had met him, Sergeant Strickland cracked a smile. It was a small one, but it was a smile just the same. And that was enough for Amelia Bedelia.

Two Ways to Say It
By Amelia Bedelia

It's going like clockwork.

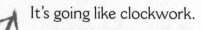

It's running perfectly.

It's as easy as pie.

It's simple.

Hold your horses!

Wait a minute!

I heard it straight from the horse's mouth.

I heard it firsthand.

Roger that?

Do you understand me?

144

Dig in.

Start eating.

Kill them
with kindness.

Be incredibly kind
to someone.

Bent out of shape.

Annoyed.

Like a fish out of water.

In an unfamiliar situation.

Turn over a new leaf.

Start over.

145

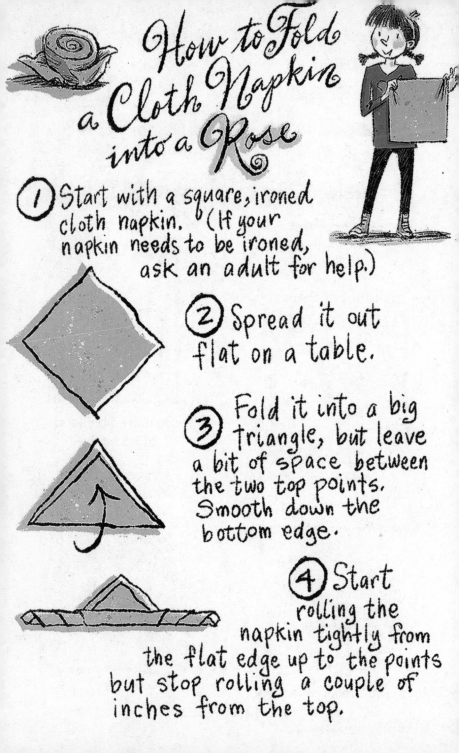

How to Fold a Cloth Napkin into a Rose

1. Start with a square, ironed cloth napkin. (If your napkin needs to be ironed, ask an adult for help.)

2. Spread it out flat on a table.

3. Fold it into a big triangle, but leave a bit of space between the two top points. Smooth down the bottom edge.

4. Start rolling the napkin tightly from the flat edge up to the points but stop rolling a couple of inches from the top.

⑤ Now take one end of the rolled napkin, and roll it toward the other end. Stop rolling at the midpoint, when there are a couple of inches left.

⑥ Take the unrolled end, wrap it once around the roll, and tuck it into the flap at the bottom.

⑦ Spread open the two points at the top.

⑧ Flip your napkin over and...

Voilà!

It's a beautiful rose!

Amelia Bedelia + Good Friends = Super Fun Stories to Read and Share

Amelia Bedelia and her friends celebrate their school's birthday.

Amelia Bedelia and her friends discover a stray kitten on the playground!

Amelia Bedelia and her friends take a school trip to the Middle Ages that is as different as knight and day.

Amelia Bedelia and her friends work to save Earth and beautify their town.

5

Amelia Bedelia and her friends save their ice cream party!

Coming soon . . .

6

Celebrate the holidays with Amelia Bedelia!

Ho! Ho! Ho! Cookies, presents, snow! It's Amelia Bedelia's favorite time of year.

Boo! Candy, costumes, shivery thrills! Halloween is here.

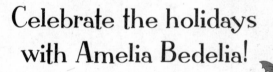

♥ The Amelia Bedelia Chapter Books

With Amelia Bedelia, anything can happen!

Have you read them all?